US MARSHAL
HARRY FINCH
DATE WITH THE HANGMAN

E. C. HERBERT

For information contact: info@palehorsepublications.com

Cover Art by Michael Thomas
Cover Design by Pale Horse Publications
Published by Pale Horse Publications
February 2021
10987654321

PROLOGUE

So far in the game of life, Deuce Morgan has been a lucky man. Accused of killing fifteen, if not more men, he has escaped the Hangman's noose every time.

Deuce, a quick tempered card shark, was known throughout the gambling circuit as a shoot now, ask questions later gambler.

All one had to do was challenge the legitimacy of his hand. If lucky, you would have a chance to recall that challenge. If not so lucky, you would weigh an extra ounce, this being the weight of one of Deuce's lead bullets fired from his pearl handled Colt Peacemaker.

You would never notice the weight gain though, because you would be dead.

Deuce got his gambling name from the first man he shot in a card game. The pot was over two thousand dollars and he won it with a pair of Deuces.

The card game had been going on most of the night. Tempers had already flared up a couple of time between Deuce and Harry "Throw Down" Reed, a well-known gambler on the circuit but not of Deuces caliber, and soon he lost nearly all his money.

Deuce bluffed a hand which caused Reed to fold. When he saw he had been bluffed, he called Deuce a scallywag. Without warning, Deuce stood up flinging his chair out behind him, drew his Colt, and put a bullet into Reeds heart.

Deuce fled, but later returned to stand trial. There were only five witnesses to the killing, and when one of them turned up dead, the others refused to testify against Deuce, so he was found not guilty and set free.

Over the next couple of years, Deuce, now with a partner, became well versed in the field of intimidation. So during trials, no one would ever testify against him, that was until Virgil Sherman. Deuce shot Virgil's brother Billy in a card game, much like all the others.

Virgil had somehow survived several attempts on his life and testified against Deuce, who was found guilty of murdering Billy Sherman and was sentenced to hang. The day before his hanging was to take place, Deuce escaped, killing one of the jailhouse guards in doing so.

A federal judge issued an arrest warrant for his capture with a reward of one-thousand dollars. This would attract bounty hunters, and because a jailer was killed in the break, it also summoned in the US Marshals with a court issued arrest warrant.

Being the western part of the country, the warrant would be issued to US Marshal Harry Finch.

Come ride with Finch as he hitches up his private railroad car and undertakes the assignment to bring in Deuce Morgan.

There are exciting turns during Harry's assignment, but as always, if you broke the law, sooner or later you would have to face your: Date with the Hangman

Chapter 1

A single shot rang out in the Silver Springs Saloon that night. A gambler by the name of Harry *Throw-Down* Reed lay on the bar room floor dead, shot through the mid-section by another gambler who will forever go by the name of Deuce Morgan.

Gone was the time he was called Henry Morgan, who was at one time a happy go lucky kid running and playing ball with his friends. A kid who let old man Hancock's chickens out of their coops as a joke, while at the same time bringing the widow Mary Stein a couple of trout he caught in the creek.

Yes, gone was the name of Henry Morgan, replaced now by the name of Deuce Morgan, gambler and killer. The name Deuce being symbolic with the pair of deuces he laid on the table the night he was called a scallywag gambler.

Deuce had grown up being called all sorts of names, and had made a vow never to let a name caller get away with calling names, especially if a name was directed at him. Deuce's father had always used the name scallywag to describe the lowest of low lives on the food chain.

"The smelly arm pits of a cowboy who had just come in off the trail not having bathed in a month," he would say. "Low life sons of bitches."

Call Deuce what you liked, but don't call him a scallywag.

Standing there now with a smoking pistol in his hand and the acidy odor of gunpowder in the air, Deuce knew Throw Down had crossed the line and he was in deep horse manure.

Deuce knew this offense would warrant more than a leather belt across his behind as punishment. He had just killed a man! Standing there, his eyes took in the faces staring at him, one being an old time friend, one he didn't know. None the less, they would point to him as the shooter, killer of Harry "Throw Down" Reed.

This outburst of anger had been escalating over the past few months. Deuce had been having a down side of bad luck drawing a winning hand and his funds were getting low enough that he was becoming desperate to draw a winning hand, which would re-stake him at the tables and the lifestyle he had come to enjoy.

Deuce had lost almost fifteen thousand dollars at the tables in River Bend, and another five thousand in Perry's Hollow. Now here in Silver Springs, he was down to his last thousand and needed the win.

Taking a brave move, Deuce played a hand he had used several times in the past when he needed a winning hand. He pulled the bluff. Now, if you gambled for a living and ended up losing a big hand to someone's bluff, why that got your blood to boiling big time, and that proved no different here.

If Throw Down had at least been able to call, the story might have had a different ending. But he hadn't. Instead he folded, believing Deuce held a higher hand then his pair of Jacks.

As is the case in a winning hand where the opponent had folded, Deuce didn't show his cards. Instead, he left them face down on the table, slid them to the pot, cupped the winnings in his hand and pulled them back towards him.

Blood suddenly boiling up inside Throw Down, he stood up and reached for the un-turned cards. That in itself an act of accusation. From that second on, the fuse was lit. Stopping just shy of turning them over, Throw Down made eye contact with Deuce.

In a silent acceptance to this challenge, Deuce eyed the cards and gave a slight nod of his head, at which time Throw Down picked up the cards. Looking at the hand, the blood that was boiling inside surfaced and Throw Down threw the hand back onto the table calling Deuce a scallywag. A poor choice for a word that would be your last one spoken on this earth, but that was what it was.

Standing quickly, his chair flung out behind him, the Peacemaker suddenly appearing in his hand, Deuce fired a round into the center of Throw Downs chest, piercing his heart. He was dead before he hit the floor.

Stunned by his action, Deuce stood there in disbelief. Waving his pistol in the faces of the others as a warning, Deuce fled the scene.

"What have I done," he whispered as he ran through the bat wing saloon doors and to the hotel where he had been staying.

Bursting into his room, Deuce threw together his simple belongings into his travel bag and headed for the livery stable and a horse. He intended on buying a horse and saddle but there was no one around so he found a saddle and horse and left fifty dollars as payment for the saddle and horse, a payment the livery owner refused to acknowledge later on, which would add to Deuce's crimes.

Coming into Silver Springs on the train, Deuce had noticed an abandoned Indian settlement, so that is where he rode. He needed time to think about what he had just done, and more so, what to do next.

I can't say I was defending myself, he didn't have a weapon, he thought as he rode.

The night air was getting chilly, and soon he could see his and the horse's breath, coming out in big white puff clouds.

"I hope there is something to make a fire with at the abandoned village," he uttered through chattering teeth, getting colder by the minute.

Deuce found one of the mud dwellings pretty much intact, so he decided that was the place he would settle in for the remainder of the night. Gathering some material to start a fire with, he set out getting one lit. Soon, he had a roaring fire going which heated up the room he was calling home for the night.

"Wish I had some coffee to boil," he said aloud.

As tired as Deuce was, sleep wasn't on the menu that night, instead his mind was filled with not knowing what to do, where to turn, or who to talk to.

"I don't want to hang," he said to the empty room. "What should I do?"

Sitting there watching the designs the flames made on the bare walls of the Indian hut, Deuce, for the first time in his adult life was scared. He knew that within the next few days, the sheriff would petition the court and issue a warrant for his arrest along with a reward, which in turn would attract every bounty hunter in the area.

Growing up in a small town where everyone went to church, Deuce knew the Lord and knew he had to talk to a preacher and get advice on what to do. The church house in Silver Springs was located just outside of town and the Reverend Richard Burr had a house right next to it. Deuce would wait till next morning, then make his way there and get some advice from the reverend.

Sleep would not come to Deuce that night. Soon it was morning and the first, *errr, errr, er, er, errrrrrrrrrrrr,* of the morning cock rooster went out into the airwaves. Deuce was saddled and ready to go. He made his way to the reverend's place.

Reverend Burr had coffee boiling when he heard the knock on his door, which surprised him being so early in the morning. Opening the door, Reverend Burr knew he was looking at a very troubled soul and immediately invited Deuce into his home where he offered him a chair and a cup of coffee.

Pouring himself a cup, Reverend Burr took a chair and sat in silence knowing that Deuce would speak when ready. Soon enough, Deuce started telling the reverend what had happened the night before.

As Deuce spoke, Reverend Burr listened intensely, noticing the new custom made leather boots he wore, the nicely fitted pants, vest, new black felt hat, and the coat he wore. Everything he was remembering he enjoyed not too long ago when he was a gambler traveling the gambling route throughout the mid-west, even taking his shot at San Francisco, before losing everything and winding up in prison.

This young man before him now, was bringing back memories he hadn't thought about in the past two years and the desire returned to sit at a table with thousands of dollars at stake in a big stake game where only the best ever entered.

I've had the clothes, the lifestyle, everything money could afford me. He thought, listening and looking at Deuce.

When Deuce finally got done telling his story and the reverend poured him another cup of coffee, offering him some breakfast also, he accepted both as his stomach was telling him he was hungry.

Bacon, eggs, and more coffee, the reverend asked Deuce. "What do you want to do?"

"I don't know, reverend. On one hand, I want to give myself up because I know there will be bounty hunters dogging my trail if I don't. But, on the other hand, I don't want to hang either, something I will probably be doing if standing trial," Deuce told him.

"What should I do? Tell me, reverend. What do I need to do to make sure these witnesses don't testify at my trial?" asked Deuce. "Seems to me when asked on a witness stand, they will tell what they saw and that was me shooting Throw Down in cold blood because he wasn't armed."

"Give them a reason not to testify, and they won't testify. That's the way I see it," Reverend Burr told him. "That's all you need to do."

"I don't have any money to pay anybody off," Deuce told him. "Do you have money you want to give me?"

"Who say's you need money," asked the reverend. "You don't need any money."

"What do you suggest then reverend," Deuce asked with a snickering sound in his voice. "Shoot them all?"

"No, not at all, but you could pay a couple of them a nighttime visit and bust them up some and warn them against testifying against you," reverend said. "The others will get the message, you see."

"I don't know any of those other fellas who were there, much less where they live," Deuce informed him.

"Leave that up to me. I'll see the sheriff today and get some of the facts he has from last night. You can stay here today and hide out, and when I know who some of the witnesses are, I'll come back then we can plan on what to do next."

"I knew if I could talk to a preacher I would get some answers. Thanks Reverend for all your help," Deuce breathe a sigh of relief. "By the way, what should I call you?"

"Let's go with Reverend Burr, and you are?"

"Deuce," said Henry. "Call me Deuce."

Chapter 2

Harry was in his living room playing with his new son, AJ, and at that moment he couldn't have been happier. He had a nice home. It was filled with the love of a beautiful woman and now his son. And as always, the aroma of freshly boiled coffee.

After the assignment to capture the Indian known as Many Lives, and what a task that had proven to be, Harry decided to take a short break between assignments to stay at home with his beloved Amanda and their new son Anthony James Finch or AJ for short. But as with everything in life, all good things must come to an end.

"I have to return to work," Harry told Amanda, while bouncing AJ on his knee. "Tomorrow, I'll notify the main office and tell them I'm ready for my next assignment."

Amanda agreed. She had noticed an uneasiness about him this past week and knew he longed to be working.

Next morning after breakfast, Harry saddled up and rode into town to his private railroad car, which acted as his office. Seeing it for the first time in several weeks brought a happy feeling to him, and the uneasiness he had been feeling went away.

"Hi old girl," he spoke aloud. "Are you ready for a new adventure?"

Unlocking the door Harry stepped inside.

"Everything looks just the way I left it," he said aloud. "Needs some cleaning up though, but first things first," he continued talking aloud.

Harry fired up the stove and filled the coffee pot with fresh water he had brought with him from home.

"That's right," he continued. "Coffee time."

Soon the aroma of his beloved coffee filled the room and Harry's mouth started to water with the want for the steaming, black liquid he had come to love. Taking the telegraph key from the closet, Harry hitched it up and sent a telegraph to the main office advising them he was ready to return to work and needed an assignment. Getting an assignment meant a new adventure to Harry and he lived for them.

Although these past few weeks with his family had been fulfilling to him, nothing took the place of being on the trail of the bad guy and the satisfaction of taking him down.

Sipping his coffee and waiting for a reply from the head office, Harry spied his trophy case filled with reminders of past assignments he had accomplished and his lips turned up in a smile.

Not one failed assignment Dad, I hope I've made you proud, were his thoughts as he sat staring into the case.

In his home, he had his father's trophy case crammed full of reminders of his accomplishments of capturing the bad guy and bringing them to justice. His body gave off a slight shiver at the sight of the two arrows. One of them broken in half, and both had three painted red circles around their centers stared back at him. They were a visual reminder of a world he didn't want to return to.

Dah-dit-dit-dah-dah of the telegraph key brought Harry back to the present task at hand. With pencil and paper, Harry jotted down the message as the dit-dit-dah's echoed in the small room. After a welcome back greeting, came his next assignment, with more information to come the message went on to read.

Seeing there would be some saddle time involved, brought another smile to Harry's face. He had the go ahead to have a smaller tag behind rail car custom built for his horse Duke, his saddle, and other provisions. This is what he had insisted on after his last assignment.

"It's important we have our own horse and equipment," he told the head office.

"A marshal had to know the limitations of his mount. Man and horse needed to be as one on the open trail. Just as pork was to beans, so was horse to rider," he had written.

Harry was a little surprised when his request was granted and the order was placed for the special rail car he requested, to be produced and shipped to Harry in

Dusty Hollow. Harry's plan meant he could easily store a two week supply of hay and oats, along with a large wooden barrel for water. There was a special harness in the stall to hitch Duke up, so he would be able to stay balanced with any movement the train might encounter.

Harry straightened his car up and made a list of provisions he needed to replace before he left on his next assignment. Little Bobbie saw Harry in his rail car, so he stopped in to see if Harry needed anything.

Bobbie was one of the town's errand runners. He would deliver items to your door as well as pickup items you requested.

"Morning marshal," Bobbie said, opening the door and stepping inside. No knock needed as he had an open invitation to "come on in" whenever he saw the marshal there. Bobbie enjoyed listening to Harry's stories as much as Harry enjoyed telling them, and Harry visualized his own son being a Bobbie someday.

Bobbie told Harry he didn't need to pay him for the errands he ran for him, like everyone else did, but Harry gave him a couple of nickels anyway.

Harry had taken Bobbie seriously the day he told him he wanted to be a US Marshal when he grew up, and Harry could see that spark in his eyes whenever he was asked questions, Harry saw that spark appear again.

Bobbie would make a good US Marshal, Harry told himself.

"Getting ready to go someplace marshal?" asked Bobbie.

"Yes I am," Harry told him. "I'm just waiting to hear back from the main office as to where that might be."

"Can I get you anything?" he asked.

"As a matter of fact you can. I was going to pick these items up myself, but now you can do it for me instead." Harry told him, handing him Harry's list.

"Want me to have Miss Barlow put these on your tab?" he asked.

"That will be just fine, Bobbie and get yourself a handful of that rock candy you like so well," then catching himself added, as a matter of fact bring me back some of the blue colored rock candy," Harry told him.

"Will do marshal," he said, taking the piece of paper from Harry's hand. "I'll be back as soon as I can."

With that, Bobbie was gone, leaving Harry alone once again.

Sitting down at the table with a fresh cup of black gold, referring to the coffee he had come to love so much, he read over the message he had received.

Seeing that he would be going to Ogallala, Nebraska, Harry decided that was where he would unhitch the two rail cars and make that the center of this assignment. All roads crossed in Ogallala, plus it was a main railroad hub and had telegraph lines, so he could connect his own key.

Harry was a novice key operator as were all US Marshals, having had to go to school to learn how to read and send Morse code. Harry was thankful the agency had required it, now that it was a part of his new rail car.

Being a small area to clean, Harry made short work of cleaning and organizing his living quarter. And just in time as Bobbie entered carrying the items Harry had on his list.

"Everything is there, marshal. Miss Barlow had everything including the blue rock candy," Bobbie told him, setting the sack down on the table.

At the sound of the first dit from the telegraph key, Harry was at the table with note pad and pencil jotting down the series of dit and dah's the telegraph key gave out.

Whoever is sending this message is a really good key operator, thought Harry. *It's all I can do to keep up with him.*

Harry made a mental note to let the office know that when sending messages to the field they need to slow it down some so the whole message is written down. Harry was sure he missed some of the message, but had enough information to get started.

"Thanks again for your help," Harry said, taking the small paper bag from the sack. He removed one piece of the rock candy, then tossed the bag to Bobbie. "That's yours," Harry said.

"Thanks, Marshal," said Bobbie, then he was gone.

It was ten o'clock and the Union Pacific wouldn't be arriving for another hour. The stable boy would be delivering his horse, Duke, around ten-thirty.

Everything put away, Harry put on another pot of water to boil, then was surprised when the door opened and in walked Amanda carrying AJ. All three faces lite up upon seeing each other.

The train whistle sounded and Harry and Amanda said their goodbyes and Harry got ready to make the connection with the main train.

A half hour later, the train whistle sounded again signaling to passengers who had departed, it was now time to return to the train as it was ready to continue its journey.

Ten minutes later, the loud train whistle sounded again, this time followed by the loud pufffffffff, puffffffff of the steam engine and the screeching sound of the steel wheels as they were gripping the steel tracks, moving the train forward. Soon the puffff's were replaced by the cheuuuuuu, cheuuuuuu as the steam locomotive picked up speed.

Once again, for a few minutes at least, Harry sat mesmerized by sounds generated by the moving train and the swaying motion to his rail car.

"Boy, I've missed these sounds," he said aloud, his body rocking back and forth with the motion on his rail car.

It would be a two-day ride to Ogallala. Time in which to go over all the information he was wired concerning his next assignment to bring in a known gambler and killer by the name of Deuce Morgan. In studying what information he had, he determined Deuce had to have some help in escaping from the jail in Ogallala.

It would be impossible for any one person to orchestrate a jail break while under the watch that an inmate scheduled to hang has looking out for him. At least one, if not more of the guards had to be in on it. These were the thoughts running through Harry's head, as the train rambled on.

Harry was correct in assuming Deuce had help in his escape. His help was Reverend Richard Burr, who was once a professional gambler himself, before prison time and becoming a reverend.

On the evening of Deuce's escape, he had a visitor who was Reverend Burr.

Reverend Burr snuck in a small revolver that Deuce later held on one guard and forced another to unlock his cell, hitting them both over the head before escaping through a trap door in the floor that was used to take a prisoner out unseen, if needed. One of the guards was hit so hard his skull was cracked and he later died.

Deuce had never been this close to being hung before. In the past, he had used intimidation to scare any witnesses from testifying against him, but that hadn't worked with Virgil Sherman, the brother of the poker player he had shot dead.

The killing of the jailhouse guard is what brought in the US Marshals and Harry Finch. Once Deuce escaped the jailhouse, he made his way outside of town where the reverend had a horse saddled up waiting for him. His plan was to ride through the night and meet up with the reverend at Coyote's Lake.

From there, the two would ride together to the stage stop at Scorpion's Bend where they would catch the stage to Rapid City, South Dakota, providing everything went as planned. So far, everything had gone well.

As was the plan, Deuce made it to Coyote's Lake where he met up with the reverend. Now providing they didn't cross paths with anyone, it would be a two days ride to Scorpion Bend.

The temperature had started to drop some and before long, they could see their breath. What they didn't see were the two sets of eyes that followed them.

Coming upon a place in the trail that had been used as a campsite by others, the decision was made to stop and get a fire going as they both knew it was going to be a cold night. Once the fire was made, reverend took out a couple of cans of beans. Popping the lids off with his knife, he sat the cans next to the fire to warm them up.

"I think we should be headed south, not north, reverend," Deuce finally spoke.

"That's exactly why we are headed north," said the reverend. "Anybody would guess riding south at this time of the year. No one would expect we would be traveling north."

"I hate the cold and think we should go to Tombstone or Casa Grande. There are some good gambling tables at both places, plus it's a lot warmer there."

The reverend picked up the difference in Deuces voice and knew he was going to try to insert himself to get his way, but reverend had decided that wasn't going to happen. They were going to stick to the plan already decided on. Besides, the warm insides of the gambling halls would attract more players as they wanted to get in out of the cold.

Outside of Deuce's temper and his quickness to draw his gun, he had been having a lot of success at the tables and had joined up with a circuit of other gamblers who traveled from town to town looking for high stake card games. The reverend and Deuce took their time traveling, which offered them time to work out their gambling styles.

Being in cahoots with each other, they could play into each other's hands and manipulate the deck so as to give either of them a winning hand. As they traveled, the set of eyes was there watching and waiting. They got to be so good together they could win all the time, but had to let others win from time to time so as not to draw attention to themselves.

All would be good until someone who had too much to drink would speak out in an accusing voice and get Deuce's blood boiling, at which point he was uncontrollable. Reverend had noticed lately he was getting worse. It was like, at some point, he thought himself some sort of god who controlled who lived and who died.

Lately it seemed every card game they got into, he was more quick to shoot someone for the smallest of things and lately he had been noticing that tone of voice whenever he couldn't get his own way, and knew it was only a matter of time before he was going to do something really, really stupid.

Chapter 3

Right on time, the Union Pacific pulled into the station in Ogallala and Harry made arrangements to have his rail cars un-hitched and stored. Once done, he went looking for the sheriff's office.

Locating the sheriff's office, Harry went inside and introduced himself.

Sheriff William Caldron, better known by the townsfolk as just plain Will, was probably in his late thirties and married to Sue Ellen, who owned the bake shop. They had no children. Having a bad miscarriage, Sue was no longer able to bear children.

Will told Harry the night Deuce escaped, he had only one visitor who was a preacher and it was shortly after he left that Deuce escaped. It was because a guard named Max Morrison was killed in the jail break the US Marshals were called in.

Another guard by the name of Ned Cooper was also injured in the jail break. He suffered a head injury also, but he lived and if Harry wanted, Will would take Harry to Cooper.

"You can take me to him shortly, but first, tell me all you know about Deuce Morgan. What was his real name?" Harry asked.

"Henry Morgan. He was a professional who followed the gambling circuit. There is always a high stake game going on at the gambling emporium, The Crazy Lady. That's where the shooting took place and Billy Sherman was killed by Henry."

Remembering a couple things Harry had read about this case, his next question was, "Do you know where we can find Virgil Sherman?" Harry asked.

"Last I was told, he had left town right after Deuce escaped, but Jake the bartender might have some idea," he told Harry. "We can go and see him if you want, he bartends at The Crazy Lady."

Making their way to The Crazy Lady, they found Jake very busy. The place was packed and there were several patrons standing around one table in particular, where a high stakes game was going on.

"Well, hi Will," it was Jake the bartender's voice. "What brings you to my place?"

"This is US Marshal Harry Finch, he is here to ask you some questions in regards to the shooting that took place concerning that gambler, Deuce Morgan."

"Glade to meet you, marshal," he said holding out his hand. "How can I help you?"

"Nice to meet you," Harry said in return, grasping his hand in a friendly hand shake. "Tell me what you know about this fella Deuce Morgan?"

"His real name is Henry Morgan. He had been coming here for about four days and sat at that table right over there," he said, pointing to the table where there was another game being played. "He shot Billy Sherman right there."

"Tell me what you know about that shooting." Harry asked.

"Well marshal, I didn't witness the shooting. I was in the back room getting some fresh bottles of whiskey, when I heard the gunshot. When I came running out, I saw Deuce standing with a smoking gun in his hand," Jake told Harry. There were three others looking on. One of them being Billy's brother Virgil."

"These types of games usually go on for days. How long had this one been going on?" Harry asked.

"Three days. There wasn't one player who won a lot, but Billy probably was losing the most," Jake said.

"How was the temperament at the table?" Harry asked. "Was it friendly?"

"It was up and down. About what you see in one of those games. When you're losing thousands of dollars, tempers run high."

"What can you tell me about the others at the table?" Harry asked.

"Besides Virgil, the other two watching the game I didn't know them, they had only been here for a couple of hours."

"Who were the other card players?" Harry questioned.

"I don't know who they were, marshal. Billy was the only one who was a regular. The other players came and went, except for this one guy. He would play for a while, leave for some time then return and play some more."

"Do you know who he was?" Harry asked. "Had he been in here before?"

"No, marshal. Only thing I can tell you is when he would sit down to play, Deuce would start to win. Now, I've seen it before where two players were in cahoots with each other and between them they could control the deck so the cards fell in one of their favor."

"So, you didn't see the actual killing, correct?" Harry asked.

"No I didn't," he told Harry.

"Have you seen any of the others back in here since the shooting?" Harry asked again.

No, marshal," Jake said.

"Well Jake, thank you for your time. You have been helpful," Harry told him. Harry shook his hand, then motioned to Will that Harry was done and they could leave.

Back in his rail car, over a freshly boiled pot of coffee, Harry had Will tell him all about Deuce's trial.

"The only witness to testify was the victim's brother, Virgil," Will told Harry. "Even though there were others who saw it. Once, Virgil was almost killed and warned not to testify, or else, well they wouldn't either."

"But Virgil testified," Harry said. "I was told his testimony is why Deuce was supposed to hang."

"Originally he wasn't going to testify, but having to watch the man who killed his brother go on living became too much for him to bare, especially after someone tried to burn down his ranch."

"No one has seen Virgil since Deuce escaped?" Harry asked.

"Nope. I even went out to his ranch myself. No one was around, not even his ranch hand, Oscar Freeman."

"Did anyone else visit Deuce other than this reverend fella?" Harry asked.

"Well, I thought it a little odd at the time, but Virgil stopped by. He told me he wanted to speak to him. He wanted to tell him that he was sorry he wouldn't be attending his neck stretching because he had other business to take care of."

At the mention of the jail house visit by Virgil, Harry started to have that gut feeling that Virgil might have had something to do with Deuce's escape. *But why?* Harry thought.

"You're not thinking Virgil had anything to do with Deuce's escape, are you marshal!?"

"It's a legitimate possibility, don't you think?" Harry asked Will. "Let's explore that angle," Harry told him.

More coffee was called for, so Harry put on another pot. His mind a racing matter of brain cells!

"Are you hungry?" Harry asked.

"I could eat, Harry," came his reply.

"Okay. Let me run this by you first, that way we can both think about it while we eat, sound good?"

"Agreed." Will said.

"Let's suppose this reverend fella and Deuce were partners working together. They would have a great advantage of what cards got played and to whom. Now, let's say Billy and his brother Virgil were in cahoots with each other. Are you following me?" Harry asked.

"I'm with you, Harry," came his reply.

"Even though Billy's accusation made Deuce angry, I think he had figured it out that Billy and Virgil were playing as a team. Being as good a player as he was, along with the helping hand from the reverend, Billy sat up knowing Deuce would make the outburst that he did, so he could shoot Billy not having noticed beforehand he wasn't wearing a gun. Still following me?" Harry asked again.

"I'm still with you Harry," he told Harry.

"Now, this is going to sound farfetched but listen anyways," Harry told him.

"The night Deuce escaped, it was the reverend who helped him. Virgil was there watching with rifle in hand. His plan was to shoot Deuce when he was escorted from the jail to the scaffold. But, he saw the whole escape and he is now following them waiting for the right time to shoot Deuce himself, maybe he has Oscar with him. What do you think?" Harry asked.

"Sounds like you're digging for worms, that's for sure," Will told Harry. "But a possibility."

Having said his thoughts out loud, Harry didn't think they sounded as farfetched as he had thought. *No, as a matter of fact just the opposite.* Harry thought.

"My question is, why Virgil would shoot Deuce, if he was going to hang. He would have to know he would be caught immediately and he would be hanging also. Wouldn't he?" questioned Will.

"Because he wanted to put his bullet into Deuce like he had put a bullet into Billy," was the only answer Harry could come up with.

"Well, we can't ask Virgil because he disappeared the same time Deuce broke out of jail," Will told Harry.

"That's right we can't. So it is going to be of the utmost importance you remember every detail of what you heard, either something the reverend mentioned or something you heard Virgil say when they visited Deuce. Maybe we talk some to your guard who survived the jail break," Harry told him.

"The only thing that might be a clue of some sort was that reverend fella told me he would get in touch with any relative he could find and transport his body to the nearest stage stop and ship his body from there to wherever. That's all Harry," Will said.

"That's it then!" Harry exclaimed. For the first time, he had some sort of a lead to start with. "Let's start with the nearest stage post."

"The nearest stage stop would have to be Scorpions Bend. That's quite a ride northwest of here," Will said. "From there, you could travel to a bunch of different places because not only was it a stage stop, but the Overland's hub," he went on.

"The train doesn't run there too does it?" Harry asked.

"No it doesn't, Harry. You either catch a train from here or Rapid City," Will told him. "It's starting to get cold up in that part of the country. I would think if anything he would head south."

"He would want us to think that," Harry told him. "No, he's headed north. I'm sure of it."

"Tomorrow morning I'm going to leave for Scorpion Bend," Harry told Will. "That's where I would head if I were him."

Guess I'll find out soon enough why they call it Scorpion Bend. Harry thought. Next morning, Harry saddled up old Duke. "Are you ready for this," he whispered in Duke's ear.

Stepping into the saddle, Harry tipped his hat to Will who had come out to say 'so long.' Harry could see it in his eyes and hear it in his voice, Will longed to be riding with him.

Chapter 4

Once they reached Scorpion Bend, Deuce and the reverend had to lay over till next morning for the earliest stage for Rapid City. They had even talked about going on to Deadwood or even California.

Checking in at a rooming house called Bertha's, Deuce and the reverend split up and went checking out the different gambling parlors looking for a game and seeing what kind of action was at the tables. Deuce sat in on a low stake game just to get warmed up and to see what caliber the card players were in Rapid City, a question Deuce didn't have to wait long to have answered.

The five players at his table were novice players and low stake, no chance players here. It wasn't long before Deuce had a small pile of money in front of him and a small circle of others standing around the table watching the games being played out.

These players are me when I first started out, Deuce thought to himself.

Henry, or now Deuce as he preferred to be called, had only been gambling for two years, but he had learned his trade quickly. One thing Deuce had learned to do quickly, which some players never learn, was to count the cards played, this giving him a huge advantage over whomever else was at the table.

What Deuce was lacking in his card game, the reverend would make up for it, as he mentored the still young, hungry, Deuce Morgan. What the reverend couldn't do was control Deuce's violent temper, and he had one that was getting worse and worse and he could see another major problem boiling up inside of Deuce.

Deuce was okay until he was called a name, then he about went crazy, and depending on the name you chose to call him, you either walked away from the table or was carried away from the table.

The name 'Scallywag' was a death sentence and a favorite one used by gamblers everywhere. If you chose to use that name to call Deuce, well, it would be the last word to leave your lips on this earth.

Without any kind of warning, Deuce's pistol would appear in his hand with a puff of smoke already coming from the barrel followed by the deadly ounce of lead which usually followed a path to your chest area where it would enter pain-free as it exploded your heart muscle, instantly fogging over your eyes in death, even before your body made a gut wrenching thud, as it hit the floor.

If you were to ask Deuce what kind of a card player he was, he would put himself right at the top with his sometime idol James Butler or the name he has been related to in the history books, Wild Bill Hickok. Deuce will even tell you he had won hands of poker holding the famous *dead man's hand* of Aces and Eights.

Deuce could tell you anything you wanted to know about Wild Bill Hickok, from his beginning to that of a US Deputy Marshal, a wagon master, gunfighter, as sheriff in the western towns of Hayes, Kansas, and Abilene, Kansas, to his duel with Davis Tutt and the impending trial, where he was acquitted.

To the day of August 1, 1876, where a lowlife scallywag gambler by the name of Jack McCall, snuck up behind him and shot him point blank in the back of the head, ending his life.

There wasn't much Deuce didn't know about Wild Bill Hickok.

As Deuce was playing, Reverend Burr was busy going from one gambling establishment to another in search of the perfect game for Deuce to sit in on.

As he did so, he observed the players and noticed they were all pretty good, but not of Deuces caliber. He was so much better than anyone he had seen so far. That was, until he entered the DEAL ME IN Gambling & Dance Emporium.

Entering, the first thing to attack your senses was the overall noise in the place. Loud piano music was joined by shrill laughter from the many scantily dressed ladies running around from table to table, swirling around, showing some leg, and rubbing their excessively large bosoms anywhere they could.

This is the one. The reverend thought, as he stood just inside the door and became accustomed to the sounds in the place.

It's been a long, long time since I've been in a place like this. God! How I've missed it. These were his thoughts, when he was approached by one of the women who rubbed up against him and asked, "Can I get you something to drink?" she asked in one of the sexiest voices he had heard in a very, very, long time and he felt his heart skip a beat.

This is when Reverend Burr realized the collar he had worn the past couple of years was worn in a falsehood. He knew right now, this is his life and no matter how hard he had tried to put this life behind him, he was never going to be able to.

"Scotch," he replied. Placing a couple of coins on the tray she carried.

"I'll be right back, reverend," she told him, battering her eyes as she realized the amount of money he had placed on her tray.

Turning around, he went back outside and reached up and removed the white collar he had worn for the past two years. In doing so, the Reverend Richard Burr transformed himself into Richard Randall.

Going back inside and just in time, the bar girl was just advancing in his direction with his drink on her tray.

Extending her tray, he removed his drink.

"Jennifer," she said. "My name is Jennifer or Jen, if you prefer."

"Randall," he said, taking the drink he had ordered from her tray.

"If you need anything else Randall, just motion for me. I'll come running."

A nod of his head and she was gone. Drink in hand, Randall walked around going from table to table checking out the stakes being played.

At one table, he noticed that one of the players had a pile of money in front of him, where the others had a minimal amount.

The one to watch, his thoughts told him.

"Gonna sit and play, reverend?" the voice behind him asked.

Turning, he was facing Deuce who had been looking for him.

"The name is Randall," he said. "Richard Randall."

"They call me Deuce Morgan. Now, are you going to sit and play?"

"If these gentlemen don't mind I think I will," he said, turning to the one with the stack of money in front of and asked, "Room for another player?"

Randall received a slight nod from his head indicating the go ahead and have a seat. Catching a pre-arranged sign, Deuce asked to join the game, also. Given the once over by the dealer, Deuce was invited to join the game also.

The hands were played in silence. The only disturbance occurring when one of the bar girls came over to take drink orders. The once pile of money in front of one of the gamblers was slowly getting less and less, as Deuce started winning.

The one gambler was pretty good and might have been able to hold his own in a straight game, but this was not a straight game in the least. Randall's job was to control the way the other players placed their bets and he did that by the way he bet. No one knows what cards he held. He could bet as if he had a full house when he held nothing or just the reverse.

The only thing he had to pass on to Deuce was whether he was bluffing or not and that was easy. Place his cards down on the table he was bluffing, anything else he was playing seriously.

The next hand, which turned out to be the biggest pot so far, was nearly five thousand dollars and had drawn several patrons who stood around the table, quietly sipping their drinks and watching the action.

There were four left in the game, one having just folded. The pot was reaching upward of seven-thousand dollars. Looking closely one could see a little bead of sweat on the forehead of the once winningest gambler at the table.

After the final call and bet placed, everyone except Deuce and the one gambler remained, all having folded. Randall noticed the few who had gathered to watch the hand being played out, was now a small crowd.

As always at this point in a high stake game, Randall slid his right hand down till it rested on the butt of his pistol, ready just in case there was any trouble as he had received the sign from Deuce, he was holding the winning hand.

A hush fell around the table as the gambler slowly started to turn his cards face up on the table. Someone close to the table said out loud, but in a whispered voice, "Queen, Queen, Queen, Jack, Jack Full house, Queens high over Jacks."

The hand was called.

Again, a hush fell on the table as Deuce started turning over his hand.

The same voice called out the hand.

"Ten, Ten." The gambler's hand still showing high.

"King," came his voice followed by the sound of everyone around the table inhaling loudly.

"King," was repeated as Deuce overturned his next card.

"King," came the voice once again. "Full house, Kings high, he wins."

Two hands suddenly came down on the table top in a loud resounding clasp, which made everyone jump.

Randall had his pistol out and cocked under the table with its barrel pointing at the gambler's mid-section waiting for his next move.

You will live or die depending on your next move, were Randall's thoughts. He had been through this before, and never had to pull the trigger. This encounter would end the same. The gambler slowly stood, picked up what remained to the pile of money he once had, nodded in Deuce's direction, and walked away from the table to the bar and ordered a drink.

Gun uncocked and back in its holster, Randall breathed a sigh of relief.

"That ended quite nicely," Randall whispered over to Deuce.

"Could have been a lot different revvvvvvv," Deuce started to reply then caught himself. "Where's the collar, and where the heck did Richard Randall come from?" asked Deuce, picking up his winnings.

"I've decided I couldn't fool myself any longer," he told Deuce. "These past few days traveling the gambling circuit, I realized I was born to gamble but as a ghost partner to a front man. That front man I want to be you, just like it has been."

"What made you decide that?" asked Deuce.

"Walking into this place tonight. Seeing the sights, hearing the music, just the desire to return to a day and time when I was the happiest. When I thought there might have been trouble with the gambler, I had my pistol out and cocked under the table, just ready to shoot him, if need be. That's not what a man of the cloth would have done," he told Deuce.

"Well, it's about time you admitted that to yourself," Deuce told him. "But where did you come up with the name Richard Randall?" he asked.

"Ever since I was a small boy I liked the name Randall. So here I am, Richard Randall, better known as plain old Randall."

It was too bad he waited until now to make that decision, because he wouldn't get a chance to enjoy it. The sound of the gun shot was deafening in the bar room, but Randall didn't hear it. Instead, the whole front of his face exploded out in a mass of brain matter, bone, and blood which covered the whole front of Deuce.

As Randall crumbled to the floor, Deuce caught sight of the gambler standing behind him with the still smoking gun in his hand. He wouldn't have a chance to fire another before he was hit in the chest by two rapidly fired shots from Deuce's pearl handled Peacemaker, ending his life just like he had just done to Randall.

There were plenty of witnesses that told the sheriff what happened, no charges were brought against Deuce.

Next morning, Deuce went to the undertaker's office and paid for a decent burial for his friend Richard Randall as he wanted to be known, a name Deuce had carved on his tombstone.

Deuce now tossed around the thought and desire to go to a warmer climate, but listened to the voice of Randall inside his head and bought a stage ticket to Deadwood, South Dakota.

The most lawless town in the west.

DEADWOOD, SOUTH DAKOTA

In 1874 on an expedition into the Black Hills of South Dakota, Colonel George Armstrong Custer announced the discovery of gold. And with that announcement, a migration of some 5,000 people infested the Black Hills and the illegal town of Deadwood was started.

Charles Utter and his brother Steve would lead a thirty wagon train to Deadwood from Colorado in 1876. Wild

Bill Hickok and Calamity Jane would be on that wagon train.

Deadwood would go down in history as the place where Wild Bill Hickok was murdered by Jack McCall while playing his favorite card game, Jackpot. The term "Dead Man's Hand" referrers to the last card hand that Hickok held when he was shot in the back of the head. Aces and Eights, and to this day it is still called the Dead Man's Hand.

As Deadwood grew, lots of money was made and lots of money was lost. Prostitution, opium, and the liquor trade were the main stay of Deadwood. Everything and anything goes in this lawless town.

With the women that were brought into Deadwood by Charlie Utter, Madam Dora Dufran's brothel would soon become the largest and most profitable one in Deadwood.

Another brothel run by Madam Mollie Johnson would also host some of the nicest looking prostitutes in Deadwood, she would also become quiet wealthy.

Saloons and drinking emporiums were also top money makers for their owners. Tom Miller opened the Bella Union Saloon which would be a top money maker in Deadwood.

Al Swearengen, who ran the opium trade in Deadwood, was owner of the Gem Variety Theater which was a front for his opium business.

On Charlie's wagon train were several Chinese. Wong Fee Lee would become a wealthy and prominent merchant, but most Chinese who came to Deadwood worked in the service trade or as prostitutes.

Deadwood would suffer two major fires from which many called it quits and moved on to other towns to continue their businesses.

Chapter 5

It had been some time since Harry had been on his horse, Duke, for any length of time, so the trail ride to Scorpion Bend was one of getting re-acquainted.

What a difference it makes when your backside is sitting in a saddle that's made just for you, Harry was thinking, remembering the saddle sores he got from the last saddle time he had to undergo.

It would be a good two day horseback ride to Scorpion Bend. Harry gave a little shiver and he realized the weather was changing. The cold was the one thing he disliked about his job.

"I have no control over the weather, ole fella," he said aloud to Duke, giving him a couple slaps on the neck, followed by a little scratching, which Duke loved.

I chose to live in the mid-west, were his thoughts as he listened to the constant ka-thump, ka-thump of Duke's hooves making contact with the hard trail and the creaking of the saddle, all the sounds Harry had come to enjoy about the trail.

He still hated the cold.

Harry knew in a couple of hours it would start to warm up. So until then, he gave heels to horse flanks and guided Duke into a medium trot to get his body moving some so it would start to warm up. Plus, he knew Duke liked to move at a quicker pace.

The smell of smoke told Harry he was approaching the Triple Creek Trading Post. There would be several along the road to Scorpions Bend and Harry had been told where to expect running into them.

"The first post is only about four hours out, but then it's about seven hours to the next one," Will had told him. "That will be Pop Finney's and where you should stop for the night. He makes one heck of a Venison Stew," Will continued.

"How's his coffee?" Harry had jokingly asked.

"Has a tendency to get a little thick the later in the day it gets," Will said with a smile on his face. "But still drinkable."

Triple Creek Trading Post was nothing but a log cabin where you could purchase the minimal of items.

There was coffee boiling on the potbellied wood stove, a frying pan with some leftover potatoes fried in bacon grease, and a tin holding a half dozen golden brown biscuits. Two bits and you could help yourself. Coffee, some potatoes and a biscuit, some oats for Duke, and Harry was ready to continue.

Melvin, who owned Triple Creek, told Harry that two men had passed through several days earlier.

"Just behind them was another fella who, just like yourself, wanted to know if anyone had passed through," he remembered. Scratching his chin, he finished with a wagon family of five who had passed through just that morning.

"Outside of those folks, no one else had passed," Melvin told him. "One of the two was a reverend or pretending to be one. He wore a white collar, but he didn't act or look like one," he said. "Dressed too fine."

"Did you get their names?" Harry asked.

"Nope, didn't get anyone's name, but both were dressed really well. One fella had on a pair of snake skin boots, which must have cost him a pretty penny."

Before Harry left, Melvin gave him a small sack of oats for Duke and a couple pieces of jerked beef.

"Long ride to Pop's," he told me.

"Be careful on the trail," warned Melvin. "Hear tell there are a couple highway men lurking around."

Highway men. Robbers, thieves, and in some cases rapists and murderers. The bottom of the barrel.

Harry remembered the time he had been almost killed by a highway man, but the short hairs rose up on the back of his neck and warned him of the impending danger. The trail became a safer place to travel on that day.

Harry never enjoyed taking the life of any man, but highway men, they deserved to be strung up.

You should be able to travel without fearing for your life, he always said.

As Harry travels now, having been warned of impending danger from a couple of highway men, he wasn't as relaxed as before.

His thoughts went out to that family traveling in a wagon by themselves.

Easy target for a couple of seasoned highway men.

Duke warned Harry of danger, just as the hairs on his neck stood up. He brought Duke to a halt and gazed out over the landscape looking for any movement. He saw none. Harry dismounted and continued moving forward with his pistol in hand. A nicker and snort from Duke told Harry he had heard something. Stopping, and now listening, Harry heard the sound Duke must have heard.

"What is that sound ole boy," Harry whispered in his ear. "Is that a baby crying?"

He heard it again, this time it was very easy to make out, it was a baby crying but someone was trying to muffle the sound.

Stepping away from his horse, so Harry was plainly visible, he holstered his pistol and called out, "I'm a United States Marshal. My name is Harry Finch," he said in a loud, clear voice while holding his badge up in plain sight. "Don't be afraid. No one else is going to harm you."

About fifty foot to his right, he saw a figure stand.

"Hey marshal," he said, and started walking towards Harry.

He saw the man was unarmed and when he was right in front of Harry, he saw he had been beaten up. He wore no shirt and there was dried blood on the side of his head, his left eye was swollen shut, and something that Melvin hadn't told Harry, the family was colored folks.

Taking his outstretched hand, he introduced himself as Abe Washington.

"I'm Harry Finch," he told him again. "Tell your family it's okay to come out."

"Ruthie, it's okay," he shouted out. "You and the children can come out now."

When they stood, Harry noticed the woman was wearing Abe's shirt and nothing else. Three children walked with her, holding hands.

"That's my wife Ruth, my sons Jeremiah and Joshua and our daughter Abigale," he told Harry. Ruth was doing the best she could to cover the lower half of her form.

Harry untied his bedroll, opened the blanket, and handed it to her to use as a wrap, so she could cover herself. Thanking him, she took the children and walked over to a pile of rocks where they all sat down.

"What happened here, Abe?" Harry asked, knowing dang well what had happened. Highway men.

Abe told him they were headed to Rapid City where they were meeting others and would be heading west to Oregon. They were jumped by two men who beat him up. Saying they had never seen a naked black woman, stripped off all her clothes laughing and hooting as they did.

"I tried to stop them and one hit me up the side of the head with his gun barrel."

"Did they rape her?" Harry asked, hoping they hadn't.

"No, they said no colored woman was deserving of a white man's seed so they didn't," Abe told him in a whispered voice so that only Harry heard.

"You need to get your family back to the trading post," Harry told him. "It's going to get cold tonight and you can't be out here with your wife and children."

If they started to walk right now, they could make it back to Triple Creek well before dark and the cold.

"We have no money," he told Harry.

Taking a twenty dollar gold piece from his pocket, Harry handed it to him.

"Here," Harry said, handing him the coin. "This will cover all your needs and then some. He might not have proper clothes for your woman, but he should have something warm at least."

"Thank you, marshal. I don't know how to thank you enough," he said taking Harry's hand in his. "Thank you."

"Not all white folks are like the two you met here," Harry told him. "Most are friendly and will help out others when the need is there."

He wished he could have stayed with them to see they got back to the trading post, but Harry had a hard ride now, if he was going to make it to Pop Finney's before dark and the cold.

"Highway men, Duke," Harry was once again on the trail and talking to his horse.

He was sure he would run into the pair, and coming from this direction, they would suspect Harry knew what they were all about so he needed to be extra cautious.

"Be on guard, Duke," Harry told him with a couple slaps on the neck.

His gut told him Harry probably wouldn't get any warning from these two, but would be ambushed. As he traveled, Harry kept a keen eye out for anyplace that might offer a good ambush spot. Rounding a bend in the road, Harry spied what he took to be the Washington's wagon. Perfect place for that ambush Harry was expecting.

Reining Ole Duke to a halt, Harry stepped down from the saddle. As he did, he saw a quick flash of light. Knowing exactly what it was, Harry dove to the ground.

He heard the whizzzzzing of the bullet as it went past his head.

Not waiting for a second shot, Harry rolled to a small stack of rocks and hunched down behind them the best he could. The next round fired at Harry, he was able to glimpse the cloud of smoke from the fired rifle shot which splintered one of the rocks he was hiding behind.

Harry needed his rifle which was still in its boot, strapped to Duke, who he knew was somewhere behind him, back down the trail they had just came over.

Harry had trained Duke to always run away from gunfire and that meant running back down the trail as most gunfire would come from the front. Gazing at a large boulder about two hundred feet away, Harry knew he needed to get there and get there now.

Having no idea where the second gunman was, but knowing one of them was behind the wagon, Harry drew his pistol, and taking a deep breath, fanned off four shots in the direction of the wagon while crouching low and zig zagging as fast as he could run towards that large boulder. Dirt was kicked up all around him as he was fired upon, but he made it to that rock.

His next run would bring him around the bend in the road and out of sight of the two highwaymen, and hopefully Duke would be close by. Not giving the shooters any warning this time, Harry bee lined it down the road. Again, several shots kicked up dirt at his heals, but thankfully none hit Harry.

Off to his right, Harry saw Duke standing in a small thicket of cottonwoods and raced to him as fast as he could. Grabbing his rifle, Harry turned and headed back, bound and determined to put an end to those two.

Harry didn't follow the road back, but took a route he hoped would bring him even with the wagon, and hopefully expose the two bushwhackers.

Soon he spied the wagon and sure enough, the two highwaymen were behind it, watching the road.

From where Harry was and how exposed they were, he could have shot them both. Although he wanted to, Harry couldn't even though they already fired upon him. Hiding himself and leveling his rifle on them both, Harry called out,

"You two behind the wagon, throw down your weapons and show yourselves. I'm US Marshal Harry Finch and your both under arrest."

One of the two turned in Harry's direction, cocking his rifle as he did. Big mistake. Harry already had a bead on him, so Harry pulled the trigger and watched him flung backwards as his bullet hit its mark. Instantly ejecting the empty shell and drawing a bead on the other, he called out again,

"Drop your rifle and give yourself up," even as Harry said the words, his gut told him that he wasn't listening.

Making the same mistake his partner had made, he turned in Harry's direction bringing his rifle up at the same time. Like his counterpart, he would never feel the bullet that ended his life. As Harry always did, he felt bad about taking another man's life, but in the case of these two, not so bad.

Harry made the decision to ride back and catch up with the Washington family and tell them there wagon and belongings were okay and they were only about three miles from it.

Riding back, Harry made the decision not to leave this family, but travel with them till it was time to settle in for the night, build a big fire, and leave for Pop's in the morning. At least by doing so, he wouldn't have to travel into the night with its drop in temperature.

Abe Washington was surprised to see the marshal riding in their direction and really glad when Harry gave him the news about his belongings, as well as his decision to ride with them for a spell. Returning with them to their wagon, Harry rounded up the highway men's horses and their belongings.

"You can always sell that stuff along with the horses and saddles, when you get to Pops or when you get to Rapid City," Harry told Abe. "I'll write a note in the morning contesting to the fact I shot the two and all this was their belongings and rightfully yours to dispose of as you see fit. I'll stop into the sheriff's office in Rapid City and tell him you're on the way also."

They all traveled for a couple hours before Abe told Harry they were going to stop for the night.

Finding a suitable area, they stopped. As soon as they did, Abe reached under the seat and pulled out a small varmint gun and said he was going hunting. Ruth and the children busied themselves collecting wood for a fire and unpacking their cooking pots and pans. With the first gunshot, Harry saw a smile come over Ruthie's face.

Fire started, a large pot on with water to boil for whatever critter Abe was shooting, and the aroma of boiling coffee filling the night air. What more was needed?

A short period of time passed before Abe returned carrying a large rabbit, which he handed to Ruth who immediately started to dress it out. A couple of cans of tomatoes in the pot with the rabbit would be dinner for them all that evening, along with a tin of biscuits.

Bellies full, they all turned in.

Ruth gave Harry back his blankct, plus another one in case he got cold.

Duke, having been feed some oats was bedded down for the night. Harry curled up next to the campfire, and listening to it crackling, was soon fast asleep.

Chapter 6

Harry never heard Ruth making coffee next morning, till its aroma reached his nose and woke him up. A quick coffee and Harry told Abe he needed to hit the trail.

"You shouldn't run into any more trouble," Harry told him. "Just keep moving. You'll come to Pop Finney's trading post by tonight, if you keep moving. I'll tell Pop's to be expecting you."

"Thanks for everything, marshal," he said extending his hand. "Ruthie and I are lost for the words to tell you how much we appreciate all you did for us."

"Just keep moving," Harry told him.

Saddled up, Harry tipped his hat, put heels to horse flanks, and trotted off knowing now they would be safe with those two highwaymen out of the way.

The morning was a little chilly and Harry could see puffs of white coming from Duke's nostrils. By mid-day, the sun had burned off the morning's chill and it was darn right hot out. Beads of sweat had formed on his forehead and Duke's neck shone glossy with its wetness.

It was late afternoon when Harry arrived at Pop Finney's trading post, and what a trading post it was. Pop's was a small mecca of outbuildings, each containing different businesses.

There was a bakery, an eatery, livery stable, blacksmith shop, saloon, and a saloon dance hall combination. Pop's was at its center, being a large log building selling all the wares you would expect a trading post to sell. Yes sir, Pops was something to behold in the middle of nowhere.

Pops, as it turned out, was nothing like his name implied. Just the opposite. Pops stood over six foot tall. He had a stern looking face that was quick to light up with hellos and laughter at a good story. Pops was also an ex-Texas Ranger, who wore matching six guns tied low like that of a gunslinger. Something told Harry he knew how to use them.

Pops was standing outside his trading post when Harry came ridding in. He stood and watched as Harry pulled up in front and Pops offered up a hand for Harry's reins which he handed him, Pops then tied off, and watched Harry step down.

"Howdy," Harry said extending his hand. "I'm US Marshal Harry Finch."

A broader grin could not have greeted him more at the mention of Harry being a US Marshal.

"I'm Texas Ranger Harold Finny, better known as Pops," he said grasping Harry's hand. "A bonafide US Marshal," he repeated.

"Well, welcome marshal to Pop Finney's. What brings you through here?" he asked.

Harry was about to answer when he held up his hand and said, "Stop! Let me guess. You're trailing two well-dressed gambler type gentlemen where one was posing as a reverend. Am I close?" he asked.

"You're spot on Pops. How'd you know?"

"Just a hunch and a little, no, a lot of Texas Ranger's training," he replied.

"You still a ranger?" Harry asked him.

"Once a Ranger, always a Ranger," he told Harry with pride in his voice. "The only thing that changes is being active or retired. I'm retired."

"Well, looks to me like you can still hold your own," Harry said to him, which drew another smile to his face.

"Let's talk over one of Cyrus' steaks and coffee," he said. "You must have come all the way from Melvin's and probably need something to eat. You can board your horse at the livery. For a couple of bits, he'll be well attended to."

A short time later they were cutting into the biggest steak Harry could ever remember, although he would have preferred it to have been cooked a little more. Along with the potatoes and biscuits, a man wouldn't have to eat until the next day or two even. Coffee was black and hot and the cobbler tasty and sweet.

"So, tell me marshal, was I right?" he asked, after a sip of coffee.

"Call me Harry, please," Harry said to him.

"Only if you call me Harold," he replied back.

Nodding his head in agreement, Harry answered his question.

"Yes. Those are the two I am looking for. I believe one of them to be Deuce Morgan who is wanted for murder and jail break where a guard was killed," Harry told him.

"I'm sure those two are the ones you're looking for. One was named Henry and he tried to get a card game going over at the saloon, but was told that gambling wasn't allowed anywhere at the post. He got really mad and within the hour they both had purchased a few items and headed out to Rapid City." Harold told him. "You're four days behind them."

"Four days!" Harry exclaimed. "Melvin told me they had been through three days ago."

"Melvin was mistaken," Harold told Harry. "Four days, not three."

Regardless, Harry was behind them still and hopefully this Henry was really Deuce. Harry's gut told him, he was.

"There was another rider who came through asking the same questions," Harold told Harry. "I did get his name, it was Virgil Sherman."

"Did you talk to him at all?" Harry asked.

"No, I didn't, but Stan at the livery stables did. He put up his horse there and spent the night at Ellie's Rooming House. Stan told me he was asking a lot of questions concerning those two. But if you knew Stan, well, he stays to himself and doesn't ask any questions from no one."

"Do you know anything else about either of these three?" Harry asked again.

"No, we don't ask a man too many questions, you tend to live a little longer that way."

Finishing their meal, Harry bid Harold farewell, indicating Harry was going to spend the night and pull out in the morning.

"Well, Cyrus will have breakfast and coffee on before the rooster crows," he told me. 'I'll catch you there if you get up early, otherwise, good luck and stop by again. Always good chatting with another lawman."

"By the way, there's a colored family behind me who should be pulling in anytime, will you see to it they have everything they need. They were jumped by a couple highway men on the trail," Harry told him.

"Highwaymen. Bet it's the same two I've been trying to catch. Sly they are. Been robbing just about anyone who comes through. "Don't know how those other fellas made it through without being accosted by them," he said. "Just plain lucky I guess."

"You need not worry about those two highwaymen anymore," he told Harold. "They tried to jump me, but I was ready for them. Their robbing days are over I'm afraid. Abe and I buried them alongside the trail right where they jumped me."

"Well, well, marshal. Let me buy you a drink and your room will be taken care of also," he said. "Anything more you want, just shout, and I'll make damn sure it's taken care of."

Harry was treated like royalty the rest of that night, and when Abe and his family arrived, they were, too. As the news went through the post, the atmosphere seemed to change.

"Hopefully, when word gets out, traffic will pick back up some. Travelers had been finding different routes to take to avoid them scoundrels, but now they're dead, business might pick back up."

"Let's hope so," Harry told him.

"No one would help us out with those two, marshal," he said. "I tried to track them down but didn't have any luck," he continued.

Next morning, as stated, Harold met Harry out front of the rooming house. Duke was saddled and ready to ride. Cyrus had prepared a special breakfast and the coffee was hot and black.

Ready to go, Harry said his farewells then climbed into the saddle once more to continue on to Rapid City and depending what he could find out there, maybe onto Deadwood which Harry hoped wouldn't be the case.

He had, of course, heard all the stories about Deadwood, especially after Wild Bill Hickok was murdered there. It was a long ride to Rapid City and one traveled without incident. Night was just approaching when Harry entered Main Street in Rapid City.

Harry's first stop was the sheriff's office like always. He wanted to let local lawmen know who he was and what he was in town for.

Raymond Stockweather, the sheriff, was not in his office, so Harry led Duke over to the livery where he had him fed and bedded down.

Next stop was the stage depot, but it was closed. Wanting to get rid of his saddle bags and rifle, Harry looked for a rooming house and saw several along the street. Sleepover Hotel caught his eye so that is where he went.

Sara Ellsworth, who owned the hotel, greeted him from behind the counter.

"Good evening, what can I help you with?" she asked, giving the handsome Harry the eye over.

"A room for the night and then maybe you can tell me where I might find the sheriff?" Harry asked.

"I have a room. Do you want a hot bath also?" she asked. "I don't know where you can find the sheriff unless he's at Mable's," she told him.

"Bath might be nice. I'll be back in about an hour, in the meantime I'll leave my things in my room."

"Mable's has the best fried chicken," she told Harry.

"Great! I'll give it a try," he told her. "How's her coffee?"

Her hunched shoulder answer told me all Harry needed to know.

The sheriff was at Mable's and he was nothing like one would expect.

Sheriff Raymond Stockweather was about fifty, silver hair, and probably fifty pounds overweight. He was seated with a woman who Harry thought was probably his wife or a widow woman, turns out it was his wife.

Walking over to his table Harry boldly introduced myself.

"Sheriff Stockweather. I'm US Marshal Harry Finch. I was told I could find you here," he said, extending his hand.

"Marshal Harry Finch," he repeated. "I am Sheriff Stockweather and this is my wife Rachael," he informed Harry and clasped his hand at the same time.

"Sorry to trouble you, it's just my custom whenever I enter a town while on assignment, I make my presence known with the local law enforcement."

"Well, that's a pretty good custom to have if you ask me," he said. "Would you like to join us?" he asked.

"No, but thanks for the offer, what I'd like from you though is some information, but it can wait until after your dinner. Will that be possible?" Harry asked.

"Meet me over at my office in forty-five minutes," he told Harry.

"I'll see you there," he told him. "Ma'am," Harry said turning to the sheriff's wife and tipping his hat.

Forty-five minutes to the tee, Sheriff Stockweather was at his office. Over the next hour, Harry learned all about Deuce and the death of his partner, the so called preacher, who went by the name Richard Randall and the unnamed gambler who shot Randall and who was killed by Deuce.

A complicated web, Harry thought.

The sheriff told Harry that the next day, Deuce paid the expenses to have Randall buried and then hopped the next stage to Deadwood.

"Just after Deuce took the stage to Deadwood, a lone cowboy came riding into town looking for the two. I gave him the same information I just gave you," the sheriff told Harry. "He then purchased the stage fare to Deadwood also."

"Did he tell you who he was?" Harry asked. "Or why he wanted to know about Deuce?"

"He told me he was Virgil Sherman and he had been trailing this fella Deuce all the way from Ogallala. Said he killed his brother, and wouldn't say anything more."

Harry thanked the sheriff and went back to his room and had a bath. Next morning, he, too, would be on a stage to Deadwood.

The most lawless town in the west.

Chapter 7

The stage ride to Deadwood was a rough and bumpy one. If it hadn't been for the five women on board, it would have been boring also, but Deuce had five women to keep him occupied. One called Ida, kept his attention the most.

The women were interested in his trade as a gambler when the question of, "What are you going to Deadwood for?" came up in conversation.

Deuce enjoyed sharing his tales of big stake games and even the danger of getting shot by a poor loser. A fun conversation was had by all. Deuce was intrigued learning the women were going to Deadwood to be prostitutes. Three told him they were going to work for Dora Dufran, having answered her ads. The other two were going to work for Mollie Johnson. Both were well known madams in Deadwood.

They all read ads in their local newspaper advertising for spirited, free women who were looking for a new adventure in a booming gold town in South Dakota known as Deadwood. They told him the ads were for dancers, singers, and all around pleasure girls. All five women answered the ads and were now hoping to be on their way to making their own fortunes.

As the day grew hotter, the women had no shame about stripping some of their heavy dresses off down to their frilly undergarments. Deuce felt it getting warmer too, but not hot enough to be taking off his clothes, then he got it! These women were prostitutes and they were just displaying their charms to see what his interest might be.

Any other time Deuce might have been interested, but not now. He had a lot on his mind with just having his friend and partner shot and killed in front of him and then killing a man himself was fresh on his mind.

When the stage stopped to rest and feed the horses, two of the women went off in the bushes with the driver and his co-driver. By the happy look on everyone's faces when they exited the bushes and returned to the stage, it would appear fun was had by all.

There was a stage stop at Big Pines and because of who was on board the stage, the stop took an hour longer than usual, but no one complained. Deuce even won a few dollars in a card game with a drifter who was headed south.

There were no other stops now, until Deadwood.

By the time the stage pulled into Deadwood, the women had dressed and freshened up. Word must have gotten out there would be women on board because there was a small gathering of cowboys, miners, and prospectors waiting its arrival.

In the lawless town of Deadwood, prospecting and prostitution went hand and hand. Deuce didn't realize it at that moment, but he had just stepped into the wildest place his young years had ever witnessed and some of the toughest gaming tables he would ever sit at. Deuce's bouts with his temper would get him an early grave here, if he weren't careful.

Streets were muddy, buildings shabby. Deadwood had a rough look to it and Deuce was in the middle of it all, his fingers burning to get at his game.

Deuce looked for the gaming hall where his hero Wild Bill was gunned down, the Nuttal & Mann's Saloon. There wasn't a dry place to walk and Deuce's custom made boots soon looked like any of the other boots worn by miners and prospectors.

The Nuttal & Mann was a full spot and Deuce wasn't able to sit at a table, so he went looking through the many saloons and gaming establishments Deadwood had to offer. Deuce was excited as he checked out saloon after saloon looking for a table to play at and realizing there were all these players just waiting for him to take their money.

Deuce finally found a table to play at in a little saloon simply named Saloon. The players at the table were okay players, but no way near Deuce's caliber, and soon there was a small pile of winnings before him, with a couple of bystanders watching the game. The stakes were small and soon he longed for a better place to play.

Giving the other players notice he was leaving after the next hand, Deuce played it out, then took his winnings and went searching for another game. Walking the street, taking in the sights and sounds, his thoughts went back to the reverend and how he would have loved this place.

It was getting late and there were a lot less people on the streets and in the gambling establishments, so Deuce returned to the Nuttal hoping to get in on a game. There were two tables that had empty chairs, so Deuce ordered a drink from the bar and watched the games being played at them both.

One table had more advanced players than the other, and as much as he wanted the higher stake table, he walked over to the other and asked to sit in. Getting the nod from the dealer, Deuce pulled up a chair and laid his money on the table.

The game being played was Deuce's favorite, 'Jackpots,' this being the game Wild Bill was playing when he drew his Aces and Eights hand when he was killed by Jack McCall.

I've won with that same hand, he thought to himself.

Much to his surprise, Deuce lost the first two hands. Instead of playing his game, he was half expecting his old friend the reverend to be manipulating the deck in his favor. Deuce knew he needed to snap out of it! Reverend was gone, he was on his own now, he knew the game, and he didn't need anyone.

Two raised voices from the table next to his caught everyone's attention.

Without warning, one of the two stood up, drew his firearm, and the room echoed with the boooooom that came before the puff of gray smoke and the splattering of brain and blood as the bullet found it mark right between the other's eyes.

Replacing his spent cartridge, this cowboy sat back down as two others dragged the dead man out the door, no questions asked. Within a minute the bar returned to its noisy self.

Crazy Jack Barlow, Deuce said to himself. Having his ability to read and count cards, he also never forgot a face, especially one who he had meet before.

It was shortly after he had killed his first man at the gambling tables.

Deuce had been riding the mid-west gamblers circuit, when he had his confrontation with Crazy Jack. Crazy Jack, now a gambler also had been a gunslinger and a bounty hunter.

It was in the town of Belmont Springs, Colorado, if his memory recalled correctly. *There were four of us at the table, two had just folded leaving Crazy Jack and myself. I was holding nothing, and in the middle of a bluff for a pot over a thousand dollars, I had just raised and called, leaving Crazy Jack to either put up some more money or toss his cards into the pot, losing the hand, losing the thousand dollars. Crazy chose to toss in his cards, giving me the win.*

Once he saw I held nothing, you could see his face turn a bright red. I watched as his eyes retracted back in their sockets, imaginary steam raising out of his ears. I was prepared for what was to come next.

Suddenly the table went flying with all the money and cards flying into the air. I stood suddenly, kicking my chair out behind me, drawing my pistol and cocking it as I did so. Silence come over the room as Crazy Jack and I stood facing each other with drawn, cocked pistols pointed in each other's face.

To this day, I don't know why neither one of us pulled the trigger, but neither of us did. Instead, Crazy uncocked his pistol, dropped it back in it holster, and silently walked out the door.

Remembering this now, I knew if the time came where we ended up at the same table again, he would recognize me. If Crazy is anything like me, that day when he backed down has been eating at his insides since it happened, and he will be waiting for the opportunity to do it over. But this time, with a different outcome.

Shortly after the gun smoke cleared, the place was again noisy with the ruckus that followed any gambling hall. Good news was, Deuce had started winning.

Because Crazy was a big winner at his table and Deuce at the table he played at, they soon had a small gathering of watchers. If things continued, they surely would end up playing each other and the inevitable would happen.

Crazy had already killed a man that evening, so Deuce was sure he wouldn't hesitate shooting another. Not being ready for that moment, Deuce played out his last hand. Picking up his winnings, Deuce got up to leave. That's when Crazy and Deuce's eyes met, and Deuce could see a look of recognition across Crazy's face. Not stopping, Deuce looked away and walked out through the bat wing doors and hurriedly walked from there, knowing quite well there would come a day when they would meet again.

Deuce felt good, considering. After all, he had just been playing 'Jackpots' in the Nuttal & Mann's gambling establishment and walked away alive, unlike Wild Bill Hickok. All this action had made Deuce want some female company.

Remembering one of the women from the stage, he headed over to the whore house run by Mollie Johnson for a little companionship. The companionship he was seeking came in the name of Ida Clark. One of the five women he had traveled to Deadwood with on the stage, Ida was the only blond. Being a little fuller figured than the others, Ida had caught Deuce's eye. Deuce knew Ida was from back east and answered an ad she had read in the daily newspaper. Deadwood, being the gold boomtown it was, was overrun with those men looking to make a strike and become rich. These were the wild prospectors. Some older and more subdued, most being younger and wilder, most seeking women who were short in number.

Shop keepers looking to make a killing selling their wares, saloon keepers, gamblers, and gunslingers, all males looking for the companionship of a woman.

Madam Mollie Johnson was one of many madam's running whore houses at the time in Deadwood.

Ida Clark would turn out to be one of Mollie's top three sporting girls, but for now, she was new and was charmed by the young, handsome, Deuce Morgan. Deuce was more than happy to spend the price to stay in her arms and to awake by her side, the next morning.

Next morning, while Deuce was having breakfast and reliving the night of loving, the stage was pulling into the depot. On that stage were two more women who had answered newspaper ads for dancers and barroom girls.

Also on the stage that morning was Virgil Sherman, the brother of Billy Sherman, who was murdered by the one known as Deuce Morgan.

Chapter 8

Virgil knew he would recognize Deuce, when he saw him. He also knew Deuce would recognize him, so he needed to be very careful as he went searching the streets of Deadwood. Knowing Deuce was a gambler, he figured he'd stake out one of the gambling establishments, in hopes Deuce would show up sooner or later.

Virgil noticed most of the saloons and gambling halls had a second story that housed rooms for rent, so he rented a room with a view of a gambling hall and waited, knowing Deuce would show up sooner or later.

Virgil turned the collar on his coat up and pulled his hat down low so he could walk the streets and not be recognized, should he come across Deuce.

Checking around, Virgil was told that the Gem Varity Theater was the most notorious of all the gambling dance halls in Deadwood.

A place that Deuce would probably be, thought Virgil.

Its tables were high stake, music loud and the whiskey and women were in abundance at the Gem.

Finding a rooming house across the street from the Gem, Virgil checked into a second story front room, so he had a bird's eye view of the theater and the street. *If Deuce is here in Deadwood, he'll show up here sooner or later I'm sure of it,* Virgil thought pulling a chair up to the window.

As the day wore on, Virgil soon realized he was hungry and sure could use a shot of whiskey and some of the fried chicken he could smell coming in through the open window. Thinking now would be a safe time to go out and about, knowing that the gambling establishments didn't start to get going till after dark, Virgil left his room to find a place for food, and hopefully a shot of whiskey.

Going out into the street, Virgil noticed most of those moving about were those working the mines. They wore dirty, muddy clothes, and they themselves were unbathed and unshaven.

Picking up a handful of mud, he proceeded to paint his face some, given off the appearance of being just another miner. Catching his reflection in a shop's window, he saw he was right. Heck, he hardly recognized himself.

Feeling now he could move about more freely, he set out walking the streets of Deadwood, looking for the man who shot down his brother in cold blood. Virgil had in his pocket a wanted poster for Deuce for his brother's murder and of the jailhouse guard.

His plan was to find Deuce, then go see the sheriff, show him the poster and have him picked up, stand trial, then watch him hang. Asking around, Virgil found out there was no sheriff in Deadwood, as far as that went, there was no law in Deadwood. If a serious crime was committed, such as shooting another person, there might be a trial for that person, but one held by the people and it had no legitimacy.

Don't take this wrong, there were hangings in Deadwood, just not sanctioned by a legit judge or jury.

Virgil knew now his plans just went down the outhouse hole.

Who could he get to arrest him? There wasn't a lawman in Deadwood.

Now what to do, he thought.

Virgil had to come up with a new plan, but what could it be?

The people of Deadwood ain't gonna take too kindly to a stranger asking lots of questions. That in itself could get a person shot.

As Virgil walked, thinking of what his next course of action might be, there leaning against a porch post, entirely out of place, was a cowboy. Unlike the folks he had seen so far, this one was dressed in clean clothes, nice boots, and wore twin tied down Colts around his waist.

Bounty hunter! The name went off in Virgil's mind.

Suddenly, without warning, this cowboy stepped of the boardwalk and into the street and called out in a very loud voice. "Reed."

Virgil's eyes followed in the direction the cowboy was facing and saw another cowboy dressed similar to the way he was, but easy to tell he wasn't a gunslinger, but a professional gambler. He wore all the fancy extras, billowy sleeves on his shirt, red vest, string tie, freshly shaven face. Turning in the direction his name was called from, and seeing the one who called it, he haphazardly went for his gun.

It wasn't even close, before he even cleared leather, a shot rang out and echoed through the streets and this finely dressed gambler lay dead in the muddy street. He hadn't anymore than hit the street when his body was jumped by several others. Within minutes, he was stripped of all of his worldly possessions, except the flannel long johns he wore as an undergarment.

Virgil followed this stranger as he walked to the first bank he came to. He went inside and moments late emerged counting some money, which he tucked inside his coat. Virgil knew then, his assumption of this cowboy being a bounty hunter was correct.

How does one approach a bounty hunter, were his thoughts?

Not knowing how to approach a bounty hunter or even if he should, he decided he had no other choice than to just walk up to him and show him the wanted poster and see what kind of reaction he gets. Taking the poster from his breast pocket, Virgil opened it up and approached the stranger.

As Virgil approached, the stranger noticed him and lowered one hand till it rested atop his pistol.

"Excuse me, sir," Virgil said as he approached, handing the poster in his direction and making it obvious to him that Virgil wanted him to read it and to also show he was unarmed.

The so called bounty hunter cautiously took the poster from his outstretched hand and his eye movement told Virgil that he was reading it.

When done, he looked directly at Virgil, handing the poster back and asked, "What does this have to do with me?"

Being direct, Virgil told him his thoughts about him being a bounty hunter. At the mention of bounty hunter, Virgil saw his hand grip the butt of his Colt and his eyes go black.

"He killed my brother," Virgil blurted out, hoping to ease the tension Virgil picked up on. "Shot him down in cold blood," he continued.

Virgil saw the tension leave the bounty hunter's face, and the hand that once gripped the butt of his Colt pull away.

"What do you want from me?" he asked, knowing darn well what Virgil wanted from him.

"I want you to kill him," he told him. "Can I buy you some breakfast and coffee and discuss it?" Virgil asked.

"Breakfast would be good," he told Virgil. "I don't drink coffee, affects the nerves."

"Good. Let me buy you breakfast," he said. "By the way, I'm Virgil Sherman."

Not giving out his name, he told Virgil, "They call me Two Guns."

"Deuce has a real bad temper," he told him. "Get him in a game of cards, call him a cheating scallywag, and you have a fight on your hands," Virgil told him over flapjacks.

"At the name scallywag, he will jump up without warning and plug ya. Now you know that, so you can be ready first. He's not that fast," Virgil told him. "He goes by the element of surprise."

After breakfast, he sat outside on a bench while Two Guns went looking for Deuce. Virgil had armed him with his description.

Deadwood was a large town with more saloons and gaming halls than one could count. So it was quite some time before Two Guns returned, and when he did, he hadn't found him.

Still believing Deuce would show up at the Gem, Virgil offered Two Guns his room, if he wanted to get off the street.

"If Deuce hears there is a bounty hunter in town, he might think you're looking for him and make a run for it," Virgil shared his concern.

The day grew quite warm, and soon it was afternoon and Virgil's stomach once again told him it wanted food. Just as he got up to cross the street to the rooming house where Two Guns was in his room, Virgil saw him. Walking towards him was Deuce Morgan.

Virgil tucked his head down low, so his face was hidden as Deuce walked by. Just as he passed by, Two Guns came out of the rooming house door. Sure enough, Deuce entered the Gem Theater, just as Two Guns approached Virgil's side. Virgil thought of what was about to transpire and was troubled that he wouldn't see Deuce hang.

A bullet was too quick, he thought to himself. And on top of all that, Virgil wouldn't be there to watch him die. He needed to think of another way to see to it that Deuce got his just reward for his brother's death.

When Virgil told Two Guns he had changed his mind about wanting Deuce killed like this, Two Guns told him that was too bad. Deuce was a wanted man. Virgil had the paper on him and Two Guns would collect the bounty.

"If you want to see him die, why don't we just walk into the Gem together and I will just call him out. When he reacts I'll draw on him and kill him right there," Two Guns told Virgil.

Having no law in Deadwood, Virgil wasn't going to see Deuce hang that was for sure. The next thing was to wait till he moved on to some other town and then have him picked up, tried, and hung. But that could take more time, depending on when Deuce decided to move on. Then there was Two Guns who was going to collect the reward money now.

While Virgil followed Two Guns, as he walked towards the Gem, his mind raced on what to do.

There was only one thing Virgil could think of doing.

I would need to give Deuce advanced warning, but how was I going to do that? Virgil asked himself.

As these thoughts were going through Virgil's mind, the stage from Rapid City was pulling into the stage stop. On that stage, along with three women who would find employment at one of the whore houses, was US Marshal Harry Finch.

Chapter 9

"Deadwood," Harry whispered as he stepped from the stage.

The first thing he needed to do was unhitch Duke and get him over to the livery stable for some oats and a good rub down. Next was to find a room, and a good cup of coffee. Harry was unaware he picked the same rooming house to stay in as Virgil had.

Next to the rooming house was an eatery named Maggie's Eats and the aroma of coffee along with steak was calling Harry's name. Fried potatoes and bacon seemed to be what Maggie's was noted for, not the steak, so fried potatoes and bacon it was along with a couple of biscuits, and steaming black coffee.

Harry didn't quite know where to start, because there wasn't any law in Deadwood. He had no one to check in with, nor to ask questions.

A piece of pie and one last coffee, then Harry was ready to start, only thing is, start where?

Harry decided not to expose his badge. He didn't need every two-bit gunslinger calling him out just to say they took on a US Marshal. Over the course of time, Harry had developed a knack to asking questions, without drawing suspicion to himself.

Going back to the livery as a starting place, Harry found the owner and just started up a conversation with him. Soon he had learned there was a stranger in town, but he didn't fit the description of the gambler Deuce Morgan.

Harry did learn of a professional gambler, who used to be a bounty hunter by the name Crazy Jack Barlow, had arrived in Deadwood just yesterday. He also learned Crazy Jack had killed another man the evening before.

Next stop was the stage depot. Here he learned everything he needed to know plus some. Deuce Morgan was in Deadwood. Harry also was told there was a bounty hunter in town. Thinking he was going to hear the name Crazy Jack again, he was surprised to hear the name Colton 'Two Gun' Rivers.

Colton 'Two Guns' Rivers was a name he had heard a short while back, while working another assignment.

Two Guns could only be in town for one reason, he had heard a bounty he was looking for was there, Harry's thought. Harry's thoughts were right, because he then was told that he had confronted a well-known outlaw who went by the name Reed.

Two Guns shot him down, and according to Irene over at the bank, he had already collected the reward money of seven hundred and fifty dollars.

If Two Guns learns there is another outlaw in town with a reward on his head, he will for sure go after it.

Harry didn't relish this thought at all. Although good with a gun, he wasn't a gunslinger.

Harry was surprised to hear that a bounty hunter as well-known as Two Guns was, would dare show his face in a town as lawless as Deadwood.

There would be no one to question or be concerned with if he was strung up, back shot, or whatever else one could think of.

The gut feeling in Harry's stomach was telling him to be careful with this one.

Harry also had to keep his eyes open that someone might recognize him. *After all, if lawmen were welcomed in Deadwood, they would have law and order here, but they weren't welcomed in Deadwood.*

Deadwood was a safe haven for outlaws, murderers, highwaymen, prostitutes, you name it, and you were safe here.

Lawmen and bounty hunters were not welcomed. So Two Guns must be desperate for money to come to Deadwood, or he had gone crazy. It was easier to hide a badge than a reputation. I could change my clothes, put a little mud on my face and pass as a mine worker, where Two Guns could never take his guns off. You see a person wearing two guns tied low and right away your mind says gunslinger of some sort. Not hard to figure out from there.

Harry was having these thoughts when gun fire snapped him back to the here and now.

Looking in the direction it came from, it had to have come from the Gem Theater, so Harry hurried over to it. He was right. Just as Harry arrived there, two bar patrons were dragging a body out the door and dumped him in the street. Within minutes, several others were stripping the body naked, not even leaving him the dignity of leaving his undergarments on.

In the few seconds, Harry had to observe the dead man before he was stripped, it was easy to tell by the description Harry had of the bounty hunter, Colton Two Gun Rivers, that this was him.

"What went on inside, fellas?" Harry asked.

"This fella here, why he walked into the place and some crazy ass gambler stood up, called his name, then blasted away," one of the men told him.

"Was the name called out Two Guns?" Harry asked.

"Sounds about right, mister. You know him?" Harry was asked.

"Nope," he told him. "I have heard of him though."

The body stripped, the three fellas took off into the night.

Harry needed to curb all of his marshal-being, not to go inside and arrest the one responsible but couldn't because he would quickly end up as Two Guns had. Dragged into the street and stripped naked.

Outside of his badge which he hid in his pocket, Harry looked pretty much like any ramrod passing through. As far as he knew, the only reputation Harry had was amongst his own kind, so he should be okay as long as he didn't overdo it with questions.

Walking inside, the Gem was an experience in itself. It was a saloon, dance hall, boxing arena, and the most bawdy establishment in Deadwood, where prostitutes were little more than dirt on a miner's work boots.

Prostitutes here were brutalized by both owner and patron and had a short life span. Once a prostitute at the Gem, you couldn't expect to leave to work any other place. A prostitute at the Gem, if lucky, only suffered daily beatings and rapes. The others were killed or committed suicide.

If you did leave, and some did, you could expect to be tracked down and beaten or killed by Al's men. Or not having any money to leave Deadwood, you simply died in the streets.

The Gem Theater was Deadwood, and Deadwood was the most lawless town in the west. Noticing the blood on the floor, Harry decided to ask the barkeep a question or two and see where it would lead.

After ordering a drink and placing his dollar down on the bar, Harry asked,

"Is that blood on the floor?" pointing to the red stains.

"Sure is, mister," he told Harry, taking the dollar. "You must have seen the dead guy outside," he told Harry.

"I did," he answered. "What happened?"

"Don't look over there now, but the gambler sitting wearing a black bolo hat, his name is Crazy Jack Barlow. As soon as that fella lying dead outside walked in, why, Crazy Jack jumped up and without warn or fanfare blasted him. Ain't never seen nothing like it," he told Harry.

"The gambler at the other table with the red vest on, do you know who he is?" Harry asked, pushing his luck a little.

"I don't know, mister," he said. "You buying another drink?"

This time, Harry ordered a beer and placed his dollar on the bar top.

Scooping it up he continued, "Someone called him Deuce," he told Harry.

"That miner at the end of the bar has been watching him pretty closely," was the next thing he said to Harry.

Uhmmmmmmmm! I wondered who it could be, Harry thought as he studied this figure. *He sure has all the looks of a miner or a prospector, that's for sure.*

Asking no more questions, Harry waited and watched. It was pretty apparent that the two known as Deuce and Crazy Jack knew each other. Just the way they swapped glances was enough to tell you something was brewing.

Pretty soon, the figure at the end of the bar got up and started to leave. Harry noticed he had turned his collar down and had removed his hat, which he left lying on the bar.

Pretty odd, Harry thought as the figure continued towards the door. As he passed the table Deuce was at, he stopped and turned towards him and called out his name.

"Deuce," was all he said. Once he was sure Deuce saw him, he turned back towards the door and walked outside.

Not knowing what was going on between the two, Harry decided to leave and follow this person, who seemed to know the killer Harry was following. Outside, Harry watched as he crossed the street to the rooming house Harry was staying in. Without having to register for a room, there was no way of finding out who this person was without just asking him, but Harry was sure it was Virgil Sherman.

"Hey mister," Harry called out to him before he entered the rooming house.

Stopping, he turned to face Harry.

"Who are you and what do you want?" he asked, his face taking on a cautious look.

"Somebody who would like to talk to you, if you don't mind," Harry answered. "Have a few minutes and I'll buy you a coffee," Harry added.

"Maybe," he said. "All depends on who the buyer is."

Sitting in Maggie's over coffee, Virgil was the first to speak. "Who are you?" he asked. "And who do you think I am?"

"My name is Harry Finch," he told him.

"What do you want with me?" he asked. "I don't know that name, or your face."

"You're right. You don't know me because we have never met before. But we might have something in common. That's what I want to talk to you about," Harry answered.

"I'm listening," he replied.

"I was in the Gem tonight when you called out a fella's name. Deuce. How do you know him?" Harry asked.

"As well as anybody could know the man who murdered his brother," he answered. "Deuce killed my younger brother Billy."

"Billy Sherman," Harry repeated the name including his last before ending with, "you must be Virgil Sherman," he concluded.

"Who are you Harry Finch?" he asked in an alarming tone of voice, and starting to get up from the table.

Deciding it was safe to tell him who Harry was and what he was doing in Deadwood, Harry opened up to him.

"I'm US Marshal Harry Finch," he told Virgil. "Please sit back down. I've been trailing Deuce for some time now," Harry told him. "He escaped from jail the night before he was to be hanged for your brothers………"

"My brother Billy's murder," he said, finishing Harry's sentence.

"I know," he continued, "I testified against him."

"I was assigned the case because a jail guard was killed during his escape," Harry continued. "Did you know that?"

"I did. I wanted to see the SOB hang, still do," he told Harry.

"What were you doing in the Gem?" Harry asked.

"Letting him know that he was being followed and watched. He needs to hanged. I had the wanted poster on him that I was going to give the sheriff and have him put back in jail to wait to be hung, but there's no lawman here in Deadwood, just a bounty hunter who was going to gun him down and collect the bounty, but he was killed before he had the chance."

"Was that bounty hunter Two Gun Rivers?" Harry asked.

"Yes it was, marshal, did you know him?"

"By reputation only," he told Virgil.

"Well, you're a marshal and have been trailing him for the jail guard's murder, so go arrest him and take him back to hang."

"I can't do that here in Deadwood," Harry told him. "If word got out I was a US Marshal, why, I'd end up lying in the street, just like Two Guns ended up. They don't like lawmen here in Deadwood," he informed Virgil.

"Then what's your next move, marshal?" he asked.

"If you would, Virgil, stop calling me marshal, and just call me Harry. Someone might overhear you calling me that."

"Okay Harry. What's your next move?"

"Could wait him out till he decides to move on," Harry told him. "But that could take some time."

"Well, I'm all ears, Harry. And right now I have nothing but time."

"There is a sort of law committee here in Deadwood," Harry told him. "Most crimes committed here are overlooked, except when you shoot down an unarmed man. Then the committee is called together and that person is usually hanged. Killing an unarmed man even here in such a lawless place as Deadwood, still demands action." he told Virgil.

"What good is all that as far as Deuce goes right now?" Virgil asked.

"I don't know right now, Virgil," Harry told him. "What I do know is, it's time for more coffee, then I'll figure all this out."

Chapter 10

Telling Virgil that Harry needed to sleep on this situation, he bid Virgil goodnight.

"Let's meet back here at Maggie's in the morning, Virgil, and see what I come up with," Harry told him. "I do my best thinking when I'm sleeping."

Errr, errr, er, er, errrrrrrrrrrrrrrrrrrrr, sang the morning rooster. With that sound, a new day began and Harry had no plan, because he hadn't been able to get one minute's sleep last night trying to come up with one. Slivers of golden sunlight came in through the window and lite up Harry's room.

What he thought of doing was to get a couple of the town's committee members together and introduce himself and what his assignment is and get their take on the best way to handle the situation. Harry had to put the notion of just arresting Deuce away. His life would be useless if he did.

Harry had himself quiet a dilemma, one he had never faced before.

I know who the bad guy is, where he is, yet I can't arrest him. These thoughts kept going through his mind as Harry walked next door to Maggie's to meet Virgil.

"And just what do I tell Virgil?" Harry asked himself.

There was no telegraph office in Deadwood so he couldn't even contact the head office.

Virgil wasn't at Maggie's when Harry got there. Neither did he show up that morning anyplace. Thinking that Virgil might still be sleeping, Harry went to his room and beat on the door. Virgil wasn't there. Harry went to the livery stable to check up on Duke and to inform the livery boy he would be boarding Duke for the next couple of days.

The streets of Deadwood were coming alive as miners and prospectors made their way out of town to the mines or to their claims to see how much of the yellow rock they could find that day.

Choosing to sit on a bench outside of Maggie's instead of walking the streets, Harry suddenly had a plan on what to do to capture Deuce. Right now he needed to locate Virgil before he could do something stupid, which could ruin those plans.

If I can locate Virgil, I'm sure I will find Deuce also. Harry thought.

Pulling his collar up, Harry realized for the first time the chill to the morning's air and hoped his Amanda and son AJ were warm in their home.

Harry stuck his head into the Gem Theater hoping Virgil and Deuce might be there. They weren't. Harry entered every saloon and gambling establishment he came to that were open with no luck. Finally, he stood outside of the Nuttal & Mann Saloon. The sounds coming from inside told Harry there was a lot going on.

Harry knew his presence would be known when he walked in, so he was hoping no one inside had ever crossed his path who could give him away. Harry gave a quick look around through the bat wing door before stepping inside. Although there were lots of patrons inside, the place was so large it wasn't crowded.

At the bar, Harry got a beer and scanned the floor.

Virgil was here, sitting at a table with three other players. He was crouched down over his hand of cards trying to make himself unnoticed. The majority of the patrons were standing around two other tables.

At one was the man Harry wanted, Deuce Morgan, and standing over his right shoulder was a beautiful woman who Harry would find out was a prostitute by the name of Ida Clark, who worked for Madam Mollie Johnson.

On the table in front of Deuce was a stack of money totaling in the thousands of dollars.

This was a high stake game that was pretty plain to see, Harry thought as he stood at the bar and watched the hand being played out.

The other table also had several patrons gathered around it, along with some of the bar girls and Doves who worked in the place. Sitting at that table, also with a stack of money in front of him, was the gambler known as Crazy Jack Barlow.

Their game was almost over and there were only two left playing out of four. The other player called and a hush fell over those gathered around, as they waited to see who the big winner would be.

Judging by the stack of money in front of him, Harry's bet would be Crazy Jack held the winning hand, a bet Harry would have won as the two players showed their cards. The pot of five-thousand dollars was won by Crazy Jack, and as soon as the money was raked in front of him, another game began.

Harry noticed Crazy Jack looking over at the table next to his, where Deuce was playing and had just upped the ante and called. The patrons who were around Crazy Jacks were now circling around Deuce's. Even Crazy Jack and his players had stopped to observe the final outcome to a game where the pot was in excess of ten thousand dollars.

Anyone who didn't think there was a lot of money to be won and lost in these gold boom towns was terribly mistaken. Staked claims, and homesteads were gambled away. As the game was ending, Harry saw Deuce look directly at Crazy Jack, as he turned over the winning hand. For a moment the onlookers went crazy acknowledging the winner, then settled back down as another hand was started.

Sooner or later those two would have to play each other, their egos would demand it, Harry thought, looking in Virgil's direction to get his attention to signal it was time to leave.

A few minutes passed before Virgil noticed Harry. When he did, Harry saw him extend thank you's to the other players, then getting up, he walked past Harry and out the door. Finishing his beer, Harry was right behind him, his plan now fresh in his mind having put it all together as he watched the games being played.

"Coffee?" Harry asked, not stopping as he walked past Virgil and made his way to Maggie's Eatery.

Over coffee, Virgil told Harry he had been there all night. Having looked out his window and seeing Deuce walk by, Virgil decided to follow him to see where he went and what he did.

"I trailed him to Mollie Johnson's whore house, where he went inside and emerged ten minutes later with that woman on his arm. They walked to the Nuttal & Mann together and you saw her, she was still there with him."

Armed with this knowledge, Harry's plan just got easier, but first he needed to speak with the Madam Mollie Johnson. Harry only needed a plan to get Mollie to speak with him and not sound an alarm as to who Harry was. Just how to do that, he hadn't yet figured out. Then, seeing Maggie's young daughter gave Harry the answer he needed.

"Will you tell me what your plan is, Harry?" Virgil asked. Harry could see the curiosity on Virgil's face.

"Okay," Harry said. "But let's find a different place to talk."

Just as you came into Deadwood was a large overlook rock formation, it was there they headed to. Arriving at the overlook, Harry started laying out his plan to Virgil.

"My plan is to abduct Deuce and bring him back to Ogallala where he is wanted for two murders and turn him over to the authorities there to have his sentence of hanging carried out," Harry told him. "But I'll need you to find out who the woman was with Deuce at the card table. Can you do that?" Harry asked.

"What then, Harry?" asked Virgil.

"We will go to see her boss, which I believe will be either Dora or Mollie. Once we find out which one, we will go speak to her in private and tell her who I am and that I need her help in bringing Deuce to justice," Harry continued.

"Dora and Mollie are madams, what makes you think they will help you? If anything, they will probably expose you and get you killed," Virgil exclaimed. "Why would you think either one will help you?" he asked.

"Well, I'm gonna tell them an outright lie, that's why," Harry said to him. "Now listen to my story because you are going to play an important part in it, okay?" Harry asked.

"Okay Harry, let's hear it."

"I'm going to tell them I have been on Deuce's trail from Ogallala where he is wanted for killing a family consisting of a mother and father and two young daughters ages ten and twelve. You, being the dad's brother, was hiding in the barn during the attack which left both your brother and sister-in-law dead, and their two little girls raped and traumatized," Harry told him. "Making sense so far?" he asked.

"I like it so far, Harry. By telling them a grown man raped those two little girls, well, that won't settle too good with either of them. They will want to help us."

"That's what I'm hoping for," Harry told him. "If the woman we saw him with is a regular for him, and if she will help us also, we should be able to abduct him quite easily in the middle of the night, providing he doesn't play all night and sleep all day," Harry continued.

"I think we will be able to get the help we need from either madam or the girl he is with, I would bet," said Virgil. "Especially when they hear your made up story."

"Let's hope so," Harry said.

"How do you see the actual abduction going down?" asked Virgil.

"The way I see it, he will have to be knocked out, either by gun butt or some sort of sleeping formula we can get from the doc's office. We can't take a chance on him yelling or hollering in the middle of the night," Harry concluded.

"Sleeping pills or……wait a minute!" exclaimed Virgil. "Maybe the doc will have some chloroform or ether," Virgil said, excitement showing in his voice.

"Great idea," Harry told him. "Chloroform is the one we want."

"When we get back, why don't you go find the doc and see if you can get some. I'll go pay a visit to Dora and Mollie and see what I can find out. Sound good?" Harry asked.

"Sounds good to me. Harry. Let's go," said Virgil, now anxious to get going.

Once back in town, Harry and Virgil split up, each with their own mission.

Harry's first stop was to the Madam Mollie Johnson. Mollie listened intently as Harry told his story, just as he had rehearsed it. Mollie bought it.

"The girl we need to talk with is Ida Clark," she told Harry. "If you wait here, I'll send one of my girls to go fetch her. She took the day off to be with Deuce, who was playing in a high stakes card game down at the Nuttal & Mann Saloon. I'm sure she will help out. I just can't believe any SOB could do those things to a little girl."

Ida was sent for and fifteen minutes later, she arrived at Mollie's. Harry introduced himself, but let Mollie do the talking, and within a half hour had Ida on board with his plan.

"Tonight might be the night you want to do this," she told Harry. "He's been playing since midnight and will probably play most of the day. By ten tonight, he will be fast asleep," she said.

The plan was to get her the chloroform and she would administer it. Once he was out, put a light in his room window to signal them. Harry left after thanking them for their corporation and would return with the chloroform, then leave it with Mollie, after which, it would be a game of waiting.

Feeling really good that his plan was falling in place, Harry returned to his room to wait for Virgil. To Harry's surprise, Virgil was sitting on the bench in front of the rooming house. When he saw Harry approach, his face lit up in a big smile, this telling Harry he had been successful in obtaining the chloroform. Handing the small glass bottle to Harry, Virgil instructed him on how to administer it, then Harry headed back to give it to Mollie.

Upon doing this, Harry's plan was put into motion. Harry had to walk past the Nuttal & Mann Saloon to return to Mollie's and decided to take a look inside to make sure Deuce was still there. He was. Harry noticed that there was a large circle of on lookers, gathered around the table Deuce sat at. Also seated at that table was Crazy Jack Barlow.

Harry ordered a drink then went to join those watching the game. All four players were still in and the pot, he was told, was over seventeen-thousand dollars. The hand was called and the moment arrived to see who would be the winner.

As the players turned over their cards, there was silence in the room. All cards turn over, the winner of the largest pot Harry ever saw was Deuce Morgan.

Harry had stepped up next to Crazy Jack and for some reason read what was about to transpire at the table.

Deuce, with a smug look on his face directed at Crazy Jack, reached for the pile of money in the center of the table. As he did, Crazy Jack made a movement for his pistol starting to stand at the same time. Before any violence came about, Harry had his pistol out and let it come crashing down on the back of Crazy's head, knocking him unconscious.

Without any fanfare, Harry holstered his pistol, made eye contact with Deuce who nodded his head in thanks. Then Harry turned and left the saloon, having saved Deuce's life only to take him back to Ogallala for his:

Date with the Hangman

EPILOGUE

The plan to capture Deuce Morgan that Harry had come up with, went off beautifully.

Ida had been correct. By ten o'clock that evening, Deuce was fast asleep. By midnight, he was tied face down across the back of a horse headed for Ogallala. By the time Deuce started to wake from his drug induced sleep, he had been tied down across the horse's back for four hours, and his whole body hurt.

When the chloroform wore off, Deuce would have a bad headache. But for now all he could think of was where in the tarn-nations am I.

Calling out, Deuce got Harry's attention, so Harry reined his mount Duke to a halt, and Virgil did the same. Being four hours out from Deadwood, Harry told Virgil to look for some firewood, so they could get warm and also warm up one of the glass jugs of coffee Maggie had given him.

Pulling Deuce off his horse, Harry sat him next to the fire.

"It's you," Deuce exclaimed. "You're the one who hit Crazy Jack over the head in the Nuttal & Mann Saloon, tonight," he said, his voice sounding like a drunk's.

"Who are you and what am I doing here?" he asked.

"I'm US Marshal Harry Finch and this is Virgil Sherman," Harry told him. "And you're Deuce Morgan also known as Henry Morgan. You're under arrest for murder and jail break in Ogallala, Nebraska."

"You shot my brother Billy down in cold blood and tried to kill me you S.O.B. You escaped the hangman's noose once, you won't again," an angry Virgil said to him.

They caught the stage at Big Pines to Rapid City, then it was horseback all the way back to Ogallala. Harry enjoyed seeing his ranger friend, Harold, when they arrived at Pop Finney's Trading Post.

Harry was never happier than he was, when they finally arrived back in Ogallala and he was able to turn custody of Deuce Morgan over to Sheriff Caldron.

Harry didn't stay for the hanging, he didn't have to. Harry knew Virgil was there to make sure Deuce Morgan would finally get his: Date with the Hangman